For my newest little grandson, with love

—N. V. L.

For Flazie and Emma

—B. P.

Atheneum Books for Young Readers
An imprint of Simon & Schuster Children's Publishing Division
1230 Avenue of the Americas
New York, New York 10020
Text copyright © 2003 by Nancy Van Laan
Illustrations copyright © 2003 by Bernadette Pons Fudym
Book design by Daniel Roode
The text of this book is set in Spectrum.
The illustrations are rendered in watercolor and soft pastel.
Manufactured in China
First Edition
1 2 3 4 5 6 7 8 9 10

Library of Congress Cataloging-in-Publication Data
Van Laan, Nancy.
Scrubba dub / by Nancy Van Laan ; illustrated by Bernadette Pons.
p. cm.
"An Anne Schwartz book."
Sequel to: Tickle tum.
Summary: Mama Bunny tries to bathe her energetic toddler.
ISBN 0-689-84459-X
[1. Baths—Fiction. 2. Toddlers—Fiction. 3. Mother and child—
Fiction. 4. Rabbits—Fiction. 5. Stories in rhyme.] I. Fudym,
Bernadette Pons, ill. II. Title.
PZ8.3.V47 Sc 2003
[E]—dc21   2001022950

scrubba dub

by Nancy Van Laan

illustrations by Bernadette Pons

An Anne Schwartz Book
ATHENEUM BOOKS FOR YOUNG READERS
New York   London   Toronto   Sydney   Singapore

Ewww yuck
sticka stuck!
Off goes romper suit
tug tug pull.
Off go sneaker sneaks,
tubba tub's full.

Picka toy
not the cat.
Pick another—
patta *scat*.

Scrubba dub dubba

squigga giggle squash.

Splash

splish

splish

splosh

time to wash.

Washy nosie
washy toesies

washy anything
that growsies.

Skootch down
scrunch your eyes

rinsa-rinse away.

Tippitta tugboat dippitta toots.

Yahoo! Time to play.

Scrubba dub dubba
squigga giggle squish

Splash splosh splosh splish flipsy as a fish.

Over under
under over—
whoops!

Upside down.

What a fantabulous

bubblesome doo.

Peek in the mirror.

Is that you?

Yikes, the eye.
Dabbadab dry.

Pour water in a cup.

Double bubbles bubble up.
Kicka flop.
Poke. Pop!

Scrubba dub dubba
squigga wiggle whirl.

Pull out the drain plug,
round the toys twirl.

Out you go, little fish,
rolla rolla dry.
Hugga hugga
squirmy worm.
Oh, no. Oh, my.

Another messy?

Yessee.